T0406038

of related interest

Me and My Dysphoria Monster
An Empowering Story to Help Children with Gender Dysphoria
Laura Kate Dale
Illustrated by Ang Hui Qing
ISBN 978 1 83997 092 4
eISBN 978 1 83997 093 1

Rainbows, Unicorns, and Triangles
Queer Symbols Throughout History
Illustrated by Jem Milton
ISBN 978 1 80501 041 8
eISBN 978 1 80501 044 9

Pride and Joy
A Story About Becoming an LGBTQIA+ Ally
Frank J. Sileo and Kate Lum-Potvin
Foreword by Vanessa Williams
Illustrated by Emmi Smid
ISBN 978 1 83997 526 4
eISBN 978 1 83997 527 1

Just Like Queen Esther

Kerry Olitzky and Ari Moffic

Illustrated by Rena Yehuda Newman

Jessica Kingsley Publishers
London and Philadelphia

First published in Great Britain in 2025 by Jessica Kingsley Publishers
An imprint of John Murray Press

1

Copyright © Kerry Olitzky and Ari Moffic 2025
Illustration copyright © Rena Yehuda Newman 2025

The right of Kerry Olitzky and Ari Moffic to be identified as the Authors of the Work has been
asserted by them in accordance with the Copyright, Designs and Patents Act 1988.

All rights reserved. No part of this publication may be reproduced, stored in a retrieval system, or transmitted, in any form or
by any means without the prior written permission of the publisher, nor be otherwise circulated in any form of binding or cover
other than that in which it is published and without a similar condition being imposed on the subsequent purchaser.

The fonts, layout and overall design of this book have been prepared according to dyslexia friendly
principles. At JKP we aim to make our books' content accessible to as many readers as possible.

The image on page 29 of this book can be downloaded for personal use with this program, but may
not be reproduced for any other purposes without the permission of the publisher.

A CIP catalogue record for this title is available from the British Library and the Library of Congress

ISBN 978 1 80501 306 8
eISBN 978 1 80501 307 5

Printed and bound in China by Leo Paper Products Ltd

Jessica Kingsley Publishers' policy is to use papers that are natural, renewable and recyclable products
and made from wood grown in sustainable forests. The logging and manufacturing processes are
expected to conform to the environmental regulations of the country of origin.

Jessica Kingsley Publishers
Carmelite House
50 Victoria Embankment
London EC4Y 0DZ

www.jkp.com

John Murray Press
Part of Hodder & Stoughton Limited
An Hachette UK Company

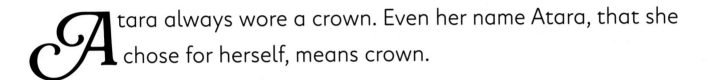

*A*tara always wore a crown. Even her name Atara, that she chose for herself, means crown.

She wore her crown to the library.

She wore her crown to the dentist.

She wore her crown to swim lessons.

At school, Atara wore her crown, lining up in gym with the other girls.

When she made a basket,
she wore her crown.

On Saturday night, when they had time to savor a book, Atara snuggled in bed with her mom.

"Atara, I bought you a new book about Purim. The hero of the story is a queen, named Esther, and she always wore her crown," explained her mom.

Mom read, "In ancient Persia, there was a king named Ahasuerus. One day, the king chose Esther as his new queen, because she was beautiful. But the king didn't know Esther was Jewish. She was afraid to tell him, because Ahasuerus's closest helper Haman didn't want any Jews in the kingdom."

"Esther's uncle Mordechai told her to invite Haman and the king to a fancy dinner and reveal her Jewish identity. The king loved Esther and saved all the Jewish people!"

After hearing the story, Atara confessed, "Mom, like Esther, I hid something—from you and Dad. I was afraid when I told you that I am really a girl, not a boy like you thought."

Atara said, "Esther always wore her crown. It showed everyone she was the queen. My crown shows everyone that I am a girl."

"You can't sleep in it! It has to stay on your nightstand until morning," said her mom.

That night, Atara dreamt of beautiful Queen Esther in her long flowing dress and a golden crown.

In the morning, Atara heard her mom enter her room.

"Time to wake up, Atara," said Mom.

Atara, already awake and dressed, responded, "Oh, I'm not Atara.
I'm Queen Esther."

At the kitchen table, Atara called out in her best queen's voice, "Mom, please bring me some royal orange juice. I have been invited to a banquet at noon, and I must have time to get ready!"

"Queen Esther, will you at least come with me to the grocery store on your way to the banquet?" said her mom, smiling.

While in the checkout line, the cashier said, "Good morning, Princess!"

"Oh, I'm not a princess," Atara responded. "I'm Queen Esther."

"Who is Queen Esther?" asked the cashier.

"She is a Jewish hero, from the holiday of Purim," explained Atara.

"Well, now I see. With that crown, you certainly do look like a queen."

As Atara and Mom unpacked the groceries, Atara asked, "Mom, do you think Queen Esther gave the king any clues that she was Jewish?"

Mom said, "No, I think it was a surprise."

In her room, Atara thought about the clues that she had given her parents. Did she surprise them?

Atara rushed back to the kitchen and asked, "Mom, were you surprised when I told you I'm a girl?"

Mom responded, "We saw your dress-up and what you like to do. But we didn't know until you told us."

Atara said, "That was the day we went to get new clothes at the store where I spotted my crown!"

Atara's mom said to her, "Your drama class starts this afternoon. Your crown will be perfect, because I know that you'll be putting on the Purim play! And the teacher is from your school."

Atara cheered as they got into the car and then they drove away.

When Atara got to class, the teacher handed out parts. She told Atara, "I've chosen you to be Queen Esther, because you already wear a crown all the time."

During the rehearsals for drama class, Atara said all her lines and did all the moves she had practiced. It was really hard to keep her crown steady. But none of the kids laughed at her.

Finally, it was the day of the performance. Lots of people came to see the show.

Atara was worried that the audience would think she wasn't a real girl and shouldn't be playing Queen Esther. But then she felt the crown on her head. That gave her the confidence she needed.

Everyone clapped for Atara after the performance. She was so proud of herself. Afterwards, Atara's mom gave her flowers.

On the way to school the next morning, Atara shouted to her mom from the back seat, "Stop the car. I forgot my crown. I can't go to school without my crown."

Atara's mom pulled the car over to the side of the road. "I'm sorry, Atara, there's no time to go back home," Mom said. "Can you make a paper crown when you get to school?"

"No," answered Atara. "It won't be like my real crown."

Atara thought to herself, "Can I really be like Queen Esther even if I don't look like her today? Will my teacher and friends still remember who I am?"

But when she got to school, kids she didn't know had heard about the Purim play and gave her high fives and fist bumps!

Everyone wanted to sit next to her at lunch.

Atara realized that she had gone the whole day without her crown. She looked in the mirror and thought she saw Queen Esther smiling back at her.

When Atara's mom came to pick her up from school, Atara skipped toward the car. Her mom called out,

"How'd it go today without your crown?"

Atara replied confidently, "I don't need it anymore. I'm royal enough as me."

Create your own crown!

Design and color in a crown of your own using the template on the next page. You can even cut it out if you'd like!

Or download a blank copy to print and cut from www.jkp.com/catalogue/book/9781805013068